C

LITTLE PEOPLE
OF THE NIGHT

LITTLE PEOPLE

OF THE NIGHT

STORY AND PICTURES BY LAURA BANNON

HOUGHTON MIFFLIN COMPANY BOSTON

THE RIVERSIDE PRESS CAMBRIDGE 1963

THE SOFT GRAY NIGHT
crept into the meadow.

The hen climbed into a
berry bush and tucked her
head under her wing.

The cow and the calf
slept under the oak tree.
They used each other for
a pillow.

The cat curled up on a
branch and closed one eye.

By now little Joe was sound
asleep in his snug bed. And the
night had turned dark and still.

But in the middle of the night little Joe woke up. He heard sounds coming from the meadow. He heard a scratching and a squealing and a growling.

Who was making all those awful sounds?

Who stayed awake when it was time to sleep?

The next day Joe took a walk in the meadow. He met the hen and asked, "What happened out here last night? I heard a scratching and a squealing and a growling."

"I heard nothing," said the hen. "The night was as quiet as sleep until the rooster crowed this morning."

Little Joe asked the cow and the calf, "Did you hear awful sounds out

here last night? Who stayed awake

when it was time to sleep?

"We heard nothing," said the cow.
"The night was soft and still and
filled with dreams of clover fields."

"I know about the night sounds,"
said the cat, who happened to be
listening. "I take cat naps in the
daytime and cat walks at night."

"Who made all those awful sounds last night?" asked Joe.

"The little people of the night," said the cat.

"Little people! In our meadow?" Joe was surprised.

"You can't see them in the daytime," the cat said. "They are sleeping in secret hiding places. But at night they come out and play about."

"I want to see the little people of the night," said Joe. "I want to see them come out and play about."

"Then take a walk with me tonight," said the cat. "I'll wait for you beside your doorstep when the whip-poor-wills start whip-poor-willing."

But before little Joe heard
a whip-poor-will, Mama said,
"It's your bedtime, Joe."

"I want to stay awake until
it's dark," said Joe. "I want
to take a walk into the night
with the cat."

Mama smiled and said, "This
once you may stay awake and
take a walk with the cat. I'll put
a light in the window."

12

"A light in the window would spoil the night," said Joe. "I want to walk into a night that's all dark."

"Oh!" said Mama.
"Then I'll turn out the lights and wait for you in the porch swing while you take a walk with the cat."

When little Joe heard a whip-poor-will
he went out into the dark night. There was
the cat, waiting by the doorstep.

"I'm ready to walk into the night,"
said Joe. "But stay close to me."

"Come along," said the cat. "Don't
scuff your feet. Put one foot down
softly in front of the other as I do. Not a
sound, mind you."

"I heard the night people making sounds," said Joe.

"But those were sounds that belong to the night," said the cat. "The night people are used to them. But if they hear daytime people they hide. You won't see them but a hundred eyes will be watching you."

The cat led little Joe to a stump
near the oak tree.

She spoke in a soft purr. "Sit
deep into the shadow. Now don't
make a sound louder than a snail's
snicker."

Joe crept deep into the shadow
with the cat.

A fat moon
climbed up the
sky behind the
black oak.

There was the
hen, sleeping in
the berry bush.

There were the
cow and the
calf, sleeping
as still as stones
under the tree.

It was quiet
enough to hear
grass grow.

Then some leaves sailed down
from the tree and landed on
the stump.

No! They weren't leaves. They
were fur balls that leaped and
tumbled over each other.

"Some of the little people," whispered the cat. "Flying squirrels. They play like kittens."

Joe watched with wide eyes until the flying squirrels sailed out of sight into the shadows.

"I never knew they lived in our meadow," he whispered in the cat's ear.

A scratching and a squealing
came from the oak tree. A furry
baby crawled out of a hole in the
trunk. It scrambled down and fell
into the tall grass. More babies followed.
And the last one was smallest of all.

"Raccoons," the
cat whispered.
"It's the first time
they have come
out to play about."

"I would like to
play about with
the little raccoons,"
said Joe.

"Don't put your
mouth so close
to my ear when
you whisper," said
the cat. "It tickles."

1663

"Oh, oh!" said the cat. "Here comes Mama Raccoon. Now watch! The babies will get a scolding."

Joe saw a big raccoon come running out of the tall grass.

Mama Raccoon
growled and poked
her babies with her
nose. She was trying
to get them to crawl
back to their home
in the tree.

But the little
raccoons loved being
out to play about
in the light of the
moon. They didn't
want to go home.

"Look!" whispered the cat.
"Here comes another family."
Mama Skunk marched past
with her six children.

All the little skunks were playing follow the leader.

Suddenly a loud hoot came from the
sky. It made little Joe jump.

"That old owl!" whispered the cat.
"It's unfriendly."

Mama Raccoon heard the owl and she
was scared. She huddled her babies
together between the roots of the oak.

Mama Skunk heard the owl too. She
held her tail high and stamped her foot.

The old owl
decided it had
better not bother
the little people
in the meadow.
It flew away.

And the skunk
family marched
on in the bright
moonlight.

Mama Raccoon
hurried her babies
up the tree trunk.

When the smallest
one got tired she
carried it. And she
crawled into the
hole with her family.

The meadow was
still again. The hen
and the cow and the
calf slept on because
they belonged to the
day.

Joe blinked his
eyes to keep them
open. He leaned his

28

head against the cat. "I would like
to stay awake all night and watch
the little people," he said. "Are there
many more of them?"

"More than can be counted on the
claws of four paws," said the cat.
"But boys belong to the day. Come
on. It's long past your bedtime."

The cat led little Joe
back to the house and left
him at the doorstep.

"Thanks for waking me
for a talk—I mean taking
me for a walk," called
Joe.

"What did you say?"
asked Mama who had been
waiting in the porch swing.

"I want to belong to the
night," said little Joe.
"But I—I can't stay awake
long enough."

Mama put
Joe to bed.
She kissed him
goodnight and
said, "Now
sleep tight."

31

But in the middle of the night.
Joe woke up. He heard a scratching
and a squealing and a growling.

Who was making all those funny
sounds?

Joe smiled. He knew who. The
little people of the night were
out playing about. He went back
to sleep and slept tight.